The StoryBENCH

A Collection of Stories

**Jacob Terry Wilkinson,
Isaac James Wilkinson and
Wallace D. Campbell**

Photography by **Wallace D. Campbell**

Illustrated by **Tim Ryan**

"Grandpa has an interesting woods that is filled with wildflowers and walking trails. He put a bench under a pine tree in one shady section of the woods where pine trees create a fully-closed canopy. He likes to tell stories on the bench, so we call it the story bench. As you turn these pages, you will get to join us in sharing our adventures in storytelling. So go ahead and let your imagination run through the woods as you read."

Isaac and Jacob Wilkinson

To order additional copies of this book, contact:
Xlibris
844-714-8691
www.Xlibris.com
Orders@Xlibris.com

ISBN: Softcover   978-1-4257-8926-8
               Hardcover   978-1-4257-8960-2
               EBook   978-1-4771-6565-2

Library of Congress Control Number: 2007906865

Print information available on the last page

Rev. date: 10/09/2024

This book is dedicated to Dad,
Mom and Sparky

David, Sparky, Karen, Jacob and
Isaac Wilkinson

Index

Other books by the authors

- <u>Did You Ever Wonder? An ABC Picture Book</u> by Jacob Wilkinson and Wallace Campbell (2004)

- <u>Who Taught Caterpillars to Spin Cocoons?</u> By Jacob Wilkinson and Wallace Campbell (2005)

- <u>What Was God Thinking? An ABC Picture Book</u> by Isaac Wilkinson and Wallace Campbell (2006)

- <u>Middleton Corner</u> by Wallace Campbell (2007)

The Rattling Chain

Chapter One

A Ghost Named Reuben

Once upon a time at my grandpa's house, there lived a goat named Reuben. He belonged to my mom and Uncle Kevin. Grandpa did not like Reuben because he climbed onto the barn and his hoofs put holes in the roof. No matter how hard Grandpa tried, he could not keep Reuben off the roof. Reuben continued to jump out of his pen and climb onto the roof. He also jumped over the fence into the yard and ate Grandma's flowers and laundry. This made Grandpa angry!

Finally, Grandpa put his foot down and said, "Kevin, put that goat on a chain." This will keep him off the barn roof and out of the yard. For the rest of his life, Reuben lived on a chain. Uncle Kevin moved Reuben to a new spot every day so he could have fresh grass to eat. Reuben was very happy until one night when there was a thunderstorm. Unfortunately, Reuben was struck by lightning and died.

The next morning when Uncle Kevin came to move Reuben to a new spot, he found him dead. He was very sad and went to get Grandpa.

Chapter Two

Reuben's Funeral

Grandpa got a shovel out of the barn and dug a very, very big hole. He put Reuben in, chain and all. The chain would always be around Reuben's neck. Everybody helped fill in the hole with dirt. Grandpa said, "Let's plant a tree in the hole with Reuben." So they did and named the tree, The Reuben Tree. Mom and Kevin said a prayer.

God of Heaven
God of Earth
Bless our Reuben
Give new birth.

Grandma cried like she always did when one of the animals died. It was quieter in the barnyard after this. The turkey, chickens, ducks and sheep all missed Reuben.

The Reuben Tree grew big and tall and so did my mom and Uncle Kevin. They grew up and moved away, got married and had children of their own. Karen is our mother. Every time Kevin and Karen came home to visit, they went to the Reuben Tree to see how big it had grown.

Chapter Three

Reuben the Goat's Ghost

One day Isaac and I visited Grandpa. We climbed the Reuben Tree and Grandpa told us the story of Reuben. The wind began to blow.

Grandpa said, "Did you hear that, Isaac?"

Isaac said, "Yes. It sounded like a rattling chain."

Grandpa said he heard that sound sometimes when the wind blew, but he could never find a chain or anything in the tree to cause the sound. He said that every time he heard the chain rattle, something good happened the next day. He also said that once after he heard the chain rattle, a patch of pink lilies bloomed under the tree. One time, a flock of robins roosted in the tree and it was still the middle of winter. His favorite thing to happen so far was when a hummingbird built her nest at the top of the tree and raised her family.

Jacob said, "I can't wait until tomorrow to see what good thing is going to happen. Tell us the story of Rueben again, Grandpa." Grandpa told us the story of Reuben and how he died in a thunderstorm and was buried with a chain around his neck. He told us about planting the Reuben Tree during the funeral. He told us about the strange sound of the chain in the tree and the good things that always happened the next day. I could hardly sleep that night because I wanted to know what I would find on the tree.

Chapter Four

The Day After the Chain Rattled

Isaac and I woke up early the next day and ran downstairs to the kitchen. We were headed out the door when Grandma said, "Boys, stop. I have breakfast ready."

Grandma makes the best French toast! She always makes that for us when we visit. Grandpa always eats oatmeal, and has orange juice and coffee for breakfast. Grandma and Grandpa listen to happy music while they eat. We were enjoying breakfast so much that we almost forgot about going to the Reuben Tree.

We asked Grandma if we could be excused from the table. She said, "Yes, but go brush your teeth before you go outside."

After we brushed our teeth, we ran out the door and stood in amazement when we got to the Reuben tree. During the night, a flock of migrating Monarch Butterflies had stopped to rest on it. There were thousands of orange and black butterflies on the tree. There were so many that you couldn't even see the leaves. A soft breeze was blowing and we heard the sound of a rattling chain. This frightened the butterflies, and they all launched into flight at the same time filling the sky and looking like flying flowers.

Grandpa said, "This was the best surprise ever!"

Chapter Five

The Tornado

We visited Grandpa as often as possible while we were growing up. We didn't always hear the chain rattle when we went to the Reuben Tree, but the times we did hear it were always special. Something special always happened when the chain did rattle, however, none of the day after surprises were ever as awesome as the time the Monarch Butterflies covered the tree and filled the air when they flew away.

One time we found a two-headed turtle in the creek. Another time an indigo bunting came to the bird feeder the same day a Baltimore oriole visited. Unusual birds and beautiful flowers were two common occurrences after hearing the chain rattle.

One spring, there was a tornado in April. The Reuben Tree was ripped from the ground and carried away. We never did find the tree. I looked in the hole where the tree once stood and found Reuben's chain. It was old and it was rusty so we left it in the hole when we filled it in. We planted a new tree where the Reuben Tree once stood, but we never heard the mysterious sound of the rattling chain after that.

The Disappearing Cave

Chapter One

Discovering the Secret Cave

One day while my brother Isaac and I were walking with Grandpa along Massie's Creek, we discovered a cave. It was a big cave hidden by trees and vines. We found it while chasing toads that we were trying to catch. Isaac went into the weeds beside the creek first and then I followed. I heard Isaac say, "Look guys! There's a cave right here. Do you want to go inside?"

Grandpa said, "We better be careful. Sometime caves are dangerous."

I reminded Grandpa that we had brought a flashlight along with us so we could go inside to explore. I went in first. The floor was sandy and the walls were wet. There was a terrible smell of dead toads.

We saw a toad come into the cave. A snake followed it. The snake ate the toad. The snake went further into the cave and we followed.

Suddenly we saw a small grayish frog. The frog went into a secret passage, so we followed it. We realized that we were in an ancient tomb. There were writings on the walls and lots of mummies. The mummies were wrapped in white cloth that had green scum on it. We saw a lever. Isaac bravely went up and pulled it. The mummies started coming out of their cloths. Isaac grabbed the end of the cloth of one of the mummies and pulled on it. The mummy turned into a pile of rags. There was nothing inside.

Isaac started looking at the writings on the wall and said, "I wonder if there is any way to get out of here."

I saw a writing pen and started writing inside one of the pictures on the wall. This caused a secret passageway to open. There was a big cage in the passageway. I saw a button on the side of the cage and pushed it before I noticed that there was a serpent inside. He was big, red and had two very sharp horns on the top of his head. He had a giant forked tongue that he continuously thrust in and out of his mouth. As we watched him thrash his long body from side to side, jab his horns into the bars of the cage, and make a loud hissing sound that chilled us to the bone, we could only come to one conclusion.

He was mean! The cage opened and the angry serpent slithered out.

Chapter Two

The Big Battle

The dreaded serpent headed straight for us! We ran down another passageway, but we did not know where it went or where we were. A swirling vortex appeared in front of us. It was a time portal. We jumped into the portal and suddenly were back in Dinosaur Time, but we were still in the same cave. We heard a growl and felt a stomp that shook the ground. It was a baby T-Rex! He was coming straight toward us. We tried to stand still and act like statues. He kept coming closer and closer. He came nose to nose with Isaac. Isaac bit his nose and the dinosaur began to cry. Isaac felt bad, so he cheered him up by making a funny face. Grandpa began to sing a Brahms lullaby. "Lullaby and good night, close your eyes and sleep tight." The dinosaur went to sleep and we concluded that it was a baby dinosaur looking for its mother. We took care of him and he became our friend.

All of a sudden we heard a loud hiss and saw fiery red eyes. The serpent was back. He woke up the baby dinosaur and made him mad. He wanted to protect us, so the dinosaur bit one of the horns on the serpent and broke it off, This is how we got unicorn serpents. We began to run back toward the time portal, and just as the serpent was about to eat Isaac, we jumped inside the vortex. We were still in the cave but it was our regular time period. One very strange thing that happened was that the cave was no longer by the creek. It had moved to Grandpa's woods.

Chapter Three

Good Bye Cave

As soon as we walked out of the cave, it closed. There was now a big hill where there was none before. The unusual thing about this hill was that there was a big hole at the top. We climbed to the top of it to look at the hole. It was dark inside and we couldn't see anything, even when we shined our flashlights into the opening. We leaned way over to look inside and fell in. That was when we discovered that the hole in the hill was actually a time portal. There was smoke coming out of the top, and as we were falling we saw a rainbow at the bottom. We landed on our feet in soft sand. There was a big white board on the wall with a black marker. It said, "Choose where you want to go and write it on the board." We wrote, "Beach." Instantly, we saw a big whirlpool forming in the sand and we were transported to a beach in Africa.

We found ourselves in snorkeling gear so we jumped into the water and started swimming. Isaac pointed to a big dorsal fin on the top of the water.

Chapter Four

The Beginning of Danger

We all started swimming toward the beach. Just then another dorsal fin appeared and another and another and then another. There was no doubt that we were in big trouble and we didn't know what to do. Jacob grabbed onto Grandpa and started swimming as fast as he could around and around in circles. It made a huge tidal wave that drove the sharks back into the sea. It also made Grandpa sick. Luckily, Jacob had some seasickness medicine and gave it to Grandpa to make him feel better. All three of us made it to the beach and changed into hiking clothes.

As we hiked into the jungle, we heard a snarl and saw a flash of orange and black stripes running toward us. It was a man-eating, hungry tiger. The tiger came nose to nose with Grandpa. Grandpa looked deeply into his eyes as the tiger stared back at him. It was a standoff. They stared and they stared at each other until it got dark. A fruit bat swooped down and distracted the tiger. Grandpa won the staring contest, and the tiger angrily ran away into the jungle.

Chapter Five

Getting Out of the Portal to Go Home

It took a full night of discussions to try to figure out how to get home. The next morning we were watching the sunrise when we saw a hill on the horizon. There was a rainbow swirling around the top.

Jacob said, "I've seen that rainbow before."

Isaac yelled, "It's the time portal."

We began to run toward the hill. Isaac was first followed by me and then Grandpa. Grandpa had a hard time keeping up, but Isaac and I waited for him and helped him up the hill. We made it to the top and found the hole. As we looked inside we were sucked into the opening.

Swoosh! Our feet were in soft sand and we were again in the cavern inside the hill in Grandpa's woods. We found another sign on the wall. It said that trips in the time portal last only one day. It also said that the only way home is to find a hill with a hole in it. It only appears at sunrise. If you don't find the hill and the time portal the next day, you will be left there until you can find a hill at sunrise, and this only happens one time per year.

Chapter Six

Story Bench

We climbed out of the hole at the top of the hill.

Isaac said, "Let's rest at the story bench."

Once, when we were sitting on the story bench, Grandpa told us a story about golden daffodil bulbs. He said he dug up daffodil bulbs every spring and planted them in the woods until he had the whole woods filled with their beauty. Once while digging daffodil bulbs, Grandpa found a plant that had solid gold bulbs. He began to divide and replant these golden bulbs every spring until he had millions of golden daffodil bulbs. He was a very rich man, but no one knew where he got his gold. It was a secret that he shared only with me.

Another story Grandpa told us was about a Christmas berry vine that grew only in his woods. Every spring the vines would begin to grow around the trees. By the end of summer, they had grown all the way to the top of the trees and to the end of each branch. Just before frost, berries grew on the vines. Something miraculous happened every Christmas Eve. The berries would start to glow, and the whole woods was lit up with Christmas lights. The berries glowed until New Year's Eve, and then they went out. After that, the birds ate the berries and the vines and sang beautiful songs all through the cold, dark winter.

Another one of his stories was about an old barn that used to be on the property. Once when the garage was full, he parked his old car in the barn. In the morning he went out to the barn to find that his car had been restored to a brand new model. Another funny thing was that the car never ran out of gas or broke down. The best part of all was that when he drove the car on the road, the pavement was made new in front of him. If it was a gravel road, the road was paved. If it was winter and the road was icy and dangerous, the road became dry and safe in front of him. For years he restored cars for poor people who needed safe transportation. One night the barn burned down and he could no longer restore cars for people.

Chapter Seven

The Secret

It was time to leave and go home to Kentucky. Our visit with Grandpa was over for the summer. My dad is a doctor, and we are going to move to Florida when he finishes his job at the University of Kentucky at the end of this year. Grandpa and Grandma want to move to Florida too so they can live close to us. We want to build houses side by side so we can always visit each other. When you think about it, Grandpa can do that now. He can go out into the woods, climb the hill, fall through the time portal and write Lexington, Kentucky, on the board. Whoosh! He will be able to visit me. The only problem is that no one but Isaac, Grandpa and me know about the time portal. It is our secret, and now it is your secret too.

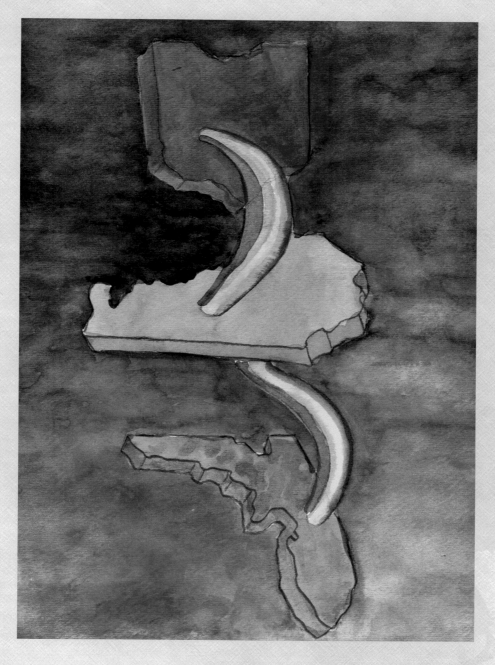

The Laughing Ghost

Grandpa and Grandma picked up my brother Isaac and me at Florence, Kentucky. We were going to visit with them for a few days so my mom could work some extra hours at the hospital. She is a respiratory therapist. Florence is the halfway point between Lexington, Kentucky, where Isaac and I live and Middleton Corner, Ohio, where my grandparents live. On the way home to their house, the discussion turned to kissing dogs. Grandma and Grandpa don't kiss dogs but everyone in my family kisses our dog, Sparky. He's a pug puppy that we recently acquired. Sparky is very affectionate and gives lots of kisses.

Isaac kept asking Grandma why she wouldn't kiss Sparky. He was persistent in trying to convince her that it is a great experience to kiss a dog. He told her you did not have to kiss him on the face, that you could just kiss him on his head. Grandma asked him why she would want to kiss Sparky on his head and Isaac said, "Sparky's fur will tickle your lips!" This made everyone in the car laugh.

At this point Jacob said, "Grandpa, tell us a story about a ghost."

This is the story that Grandpa told.

One summer the Wilkinson family went on a summer vacation to a cottage in Canada. It was secluded back a long gravel driveway. The cottage sat by a lake. You could walk out a back door onto a porch and the lake was right there. It was beautiful and it was quiet most of the time, except for the singing of the birds, the splashing of fish jumping in the lake, frogs croaking, cicadas buzzing, crickets chirping and hummingbirds humming.

Dad took Isaac and me fishing in a boat on the lake. It was fun watching the ducks swimming and the dragonflies flying around us. Before long, we were all catching fish. I caught a large-mouth bass and four bluegills. Isaac caught five bluegills and my dad hooked a turtle on his line. It was funny watching my dad try to get that turtle off his line.

Isaac asked Dad if the cottage where we were staying was haunted. He believes that ghosts are real, and sometimes he gets afraid at night even though I tell him that there is no such thing as a ghost. We sleep in the same room, and sometimes when he gets scared he crawls into bed with me. Dad told Isaac that the cottage was not haunted and that there was no such thing as a ghost.

We played hard that afternoon and decided to build a campfire in the evening. Mom and Dad let us stay up late so we could look at the sky. There was a big meteor shower that they wanted us to see. The sky was beautiful and there must have been a million stars. The first meteor we saw scared Isaac, but after awhile he thought they were pretty cool when they streaked across the sky. I lost track of how many shooting stars we saw that night.

Finally, it was time to go to bed. Isaac and I shared a room just like we do at home, and Mom and Dad had their own room. When we went to bed, Isaac started on the ghost thing and asked me if the cottage was haunted. I told him that it was not and that he should go to sleep.

I don't know how long we were asleep before we awoke to the sound of hysterical laughter. Isaac jumped in bed with me. He said, "Did you hear that?"

"Yes, I did!" I replied.

Isaac responded, "I thought you said this cottage was not haunted. I think that is a laughing ghost."

I looked at the clock and noticed it was midnight. The laughing stopped after a little while and we went back to sleep.

I had a dream that night about laughing ghosts floating over the lake. They were happy and were having a good time. They seemed friendly and nothing to be afraid of, but it was weird seeing them floating over the water and laughing hysterically.

When we got up in the morning, Mom had breakfast ready for us. She made pancakes, sausage and juice. We got a surprise at breakfast. Grandma and Grandpa had arrived during the night and they joined us for breakfast.

Isaac asked Grandpa if he believed in ghosts. Grandpa told him that there was no such thing as ghosts. After last night, both Isaac and I thought they were just as real as we are.

Isaac told Grandpa what had happened during the night with the hysterical laughter. He told him that he thought the laughing was coming from a friendly ghost.

Grandpa asked Isaac what time he heard the ghost and he said, "Around midnight."

Grandpa began to laugh until he was shaking all over.

Isaac said, "Why are you laughing, Grandpa? I heard it and Jacob did too!"

Grandpa told us that he and Grandma had arrived last night around midnight and that Sparky, our puppy, had greeted them. Grandpa picked up Sparky and kissed him on the head. Sparky's fur had tickled his lips and made him laugh hysterically!

It was Grandpa. Grandpa was the laughing ghost!

Why Birds Have Wings

Once upon a time birds had hands and walked on the ground. Little Bird had always dreamed about flying. So he walked many miles to find the Wise Eagle's tree. When Little Bird finally found it, he climbed up to talk to Wise Eagle. He asked him, "Where is the Flying Bird King's Fortress?"

Wise Eagle answered, "It's north of the Enchanted Pine Forest."

Little Bird walked late into the night until he emerged from the north side of Enchanted Pine Forest. He could see a tall, wide, glimmering castle.

Cautiously, he walked up and went inside. He saw the Flying Bird King sitting upon his throne. Little Bird bravely went up and asked, "Please, may I have wings? I have always wanted to fly."

Suddenly, his hands grew longer and began to grow thick feathers on them. Little Bird had wings! He laughed and flew all the way home to tell the other birds what happened.

And that is why birds have wings.

Shark Tooth Hunters and Tough Guy Club

Uncle Kevin and Aunt Mimi have a farm in Florida called Itty Bitty Ranch. The soil is made of sand, mud, shells and sea fossils. Uncle Kevin dug a large lake, leaving large piles of soil in the pasture. When my brother Isaac and I go to visit, we look for shark's teeth in the piles of soil. Once we even found a fossilized tusk. We challenge each other to find the largest and most shark teeth when we visit.

Uncle Kevin has large oak trees on his property. We call one of them the Thinking Tree. Its trunk branches in several directions and it is easy to climb from the ground. We always check for snakes and fire ants before we climb up into its branches. I have one section I call my office. I have decorated it with Spanish moss and air plants. Sometimes when I sit in my office, I think up tongue twisters like, "Sarasota Shell Shop Salesman" and "Pittsburg Pit Stop Tire." Try saying "Black Brass Brushed Aluminum" three times fast or Real Rear Wheel. Sometimes I make up jokes like – What is a dung beetle's favorite candy? The answer is Lolly Poops." Once I fell out of the tree but I didn't cry. I am a member of the Tough Guy Club. Uncle Kevin started the Tough Guy Club. The rules are simple: 1) Be tough, 2) Never whine, 3) Be Strong and 4) Don't cry.

My little brother is in first grade. One day he slipped on the step of the school bus. His lip was cut and bleeding and the babysitter did not want to send him to school, but Isaac told her he was a member of the Tough Guy Club and he went to school. He did not cry. My mom found him in the school clinic with the nurse.

Uncle Kevin and Aunt Mimi have lots of animals. Three of my favorites are their Boerboels, Zuri and Obie, and their Rottweiler, Rahab. All of these dogs are bigger than me and Zuri and Obie are still puppies! Boerboels are African dogs that were raised to protect the cattle from lion attacks. I like to pet the dogs when they sit beside me. I like it when they go to the barn with me to feed the chickens, horses and goats. It is funny watching them play with my dog, Sparky. He is a small pug but he thinks he is big. Sparky never gets upset when the other dogs knock him around because he is a member of the Tough Guy Club too.

Jacob and Isaac Wilkinson

Jacob Terry Wilkinson had just finished second grade and Isaac James Wilkinson had just finished kindergarten at Picadome Elementary School in Kentucky when they wrote this book with their grandfather, Wallace D. Campbell, during a visit to their grandparents' home at Middleton Corner, Ohio, in May 2006. Jacob and Isaac now live in Naples, Florida, where they attend Seagate Elementary School and are now in the fourth and second grades respectively. Wallace D. Campbell is beginning his 44th year as an educator. He is currently principal of Greeneview High School in Jamestown, Ohio.

Printed in the United States
by Baker & Taylor Publisher Services